William Augustine Leahy

The Siege of Syracuse

A Poetical Drama in Five Acts

William Augustine Leahy

The Siege of Syracuse
A Poetical Drama in Five Acts

ISBN/EAN: 9783337289980

Printed in Europe, USA, Canada, Australia, Japan

Cover: Foto ©Andreas Hilbeck / pixelio.de

More available books at **www.hansebooks.com**

The
✳ Siege ✳ of ✳ Syracuse ✳

A POETICAL DRAMA
IN FIVE ACTS

BY

WILLIAM A. LEAHY

BOSTON
D. LOTHROP COMPANY
WASHINGTON STREET, OPPOSITE BROMFIELD
1889

CHARACTERS.

LUCIUS, a young Syracusan captain.

ANTENOR, High-Priest and Senator of Syracuse; Adelia's father.

BARCA, Carthaginian general.

SALANDER, his attendant.

GYLIPPUS, Spartan general.

———

ADELIA, beloved of Lucius.

GLAUKA, in love with Lucius, a disguised Ionian maiden, Adelia's companion.

———

Soldiers, Sailors, Priestesses, etc.

———

The story is laid in Syracuse during the Athenian siege, B.C. 414–413.

THE

SIEGE OF SYRACUSE.

Act First.

SCENE I.

A secluded garden. Glauka discovered by a fountain, singing.

ACANTHE.

Acanthe carolled
    Beside the shore,
    Where the sea-maids four,
All green-apparelled,
Looking up through the waters shoal,

From their grottoes shady
Beheld her pass,
With the heart of a lass,
The grace of a lady,
And locks like an aureole;
And locks like an aureole.

Enter Lucius in full armor: he listens.

"Take thy Acanthe," —
Sweetly she sang
That the ocean rang, —
"O sister Xanthe,
Under the sparkling waves.
For thou art become
A sea-maid, they say;
Then take me away
To thy deep, new home
In the beautiful coral caves;
In the beautiful coral caves."

Where the water flows
By the old sea-bank,
They arose and sank,
And sank and arose,

Aye making a music wild ;
    While, strewing sea-charms,
      Xanthe, the queen,
      Coming unseen,
    Stretched forth her arms,
And sank with the lovely child ;
All sank with the lovely child.

Lucius (*coming forward*).   A sweet lay, Glauka.
Glauka (*starts*). Master !
Lucius.   Do not blush
Thus to be overheard.
    Glauka.   Thy plume is shorn,
Lord Lucius, and, O Gods ! this brazen plate
Is dinted like a target.   Sure it has been
The mark for many arrows.
    Lucius.   Sweet concern
And pretty wonder of thy gentle eyes !
We had a midnight skirmish.   Happy maid,
Thou, screened amid thy grove of whispering lemons,
Know'st little of the fleet that blocks our harbor ;
Nor hast thou climbed Epipolae's slope to view
Their cruel walls that like a serpent's folds

Coil round us on the land.   Just where they meet
One round redoubt is planted.   Precious blood
Anoints the meadows there : for thro' that pass
Our city's breath doth flow ; that crevice closed,
What hope for all-encircled Syracuse !
At dead of night from either wall there stole
A hundred archers and a hundred spearsmen,
The flower of the foe, all stern-resolved
To seize our coign of vantage.   But Menōn,
Our sentinel, with vigilant suspicion
Spied them afar, and touched each resting guard.
We rose, and shaking off the drowse of sleep,
As leaps the leopard from his jungle lair,
Singing *Alala!* we charged them.   Brief the combat !
Then Lamachus, the rampart of their camp,
Went down to death, and many brave Athenians
Descended with him, or since sank in flight
Among the lowland marshes.

    GLAUKA.   Shall I call
My lady ?   Nay, for she hath heard thy voice
Across the garden, and returns this way.

Enter Adelia.

Lucius.   Adelia!   (*They embrace.*)
Adelia.   This is earlier than thy wont.
Lucius.   Swift sped I, love, and blithely to my
tryst ;
While Fancy, like an eager comrade, still
Outran me, questioning, " What doth she now ? "
And " Will she meet me here before the gate ?
Or on the path ? or in her bower ?   Perhaps
She will be singing, — sighing, — at her tasks, —
Or revery-bound, watching the wingèd flocks
That, now 'tis early spring, embarking high
Upon their airy element, desert
Our winter for the North."
Adelia.   Behold them now.
O would they were the wingèd ships of Athens,
Tired of their sojourn here, and eastward bound
Back to their own Piraeus.   But no word
Of war to us, love, by my father's wish.
If thou'st an idle hour, fling down thy spear
And doff thy heavy helm, while 'mid sweet converse,
Reclining on the lawn (Remain, my dear !)
We two will give thine arms a hue of peace,
Garlanding them with flowers.

Lucius throws down his spear and removes his helmet.
They recline on the meadow. Glauka moves to and
fro, fetching flowers for the garlands.

ADELIA.   Few visitors
Disturb us, save Antenor and thyself,
And, yes, the little warbling birds that come
To tipple in our fountains.   So our life
Is pensive and severe, — unless, perchance,
As even now I heard her, Glauka carols.
Then all the garden's silent and each thing
That's blessed with ears stands trembling for delight,
Till, startled by the perfect hush, the maid
Remembers she is singing, and is still.
   GLAUKA.   O lady, what are praises from thy lips !
   LUCIUS.   Thou art a sister of the nightingale,
Fair Glauka, sweeter far than she, and shy
As, ah ! the sweetest songsters ever are.
And is it love that makes thee carol, too ?
Why not, in Love's own bower !   The very air
Exhaleth a voluptuous harmony.
Think not I mean such harmony alone
As trembles in the hearing when deft hands

Pluck music from the lyre : but such as makes
Leaf sister unto flower, and flower akin
To meadow, tint to neighbor tint, and man
Unto the zone he dwells in.   'Neath the trees
The lacing shine and shadow, — on the lawns
The light of flowers, — and from the gentle knoll,
Rough, rocky stairs descending, the cascade,
With silvery missions to the placid lake
And to the foamy fountain, — and the sky,
O'erhung with languid spreads of yellow cloud,
All laving with soft light — it is, in truth,
Love's garden.

ADELIA.   Yet Antenor heeds it little.

Lucius.   Thy father's spirit is for war and counsel,
Stern, lonely, like an Alp.

ADELIA.   But wherefore stern?
Is he not ever gentle ?

Lucius.   Thee he loves,
But he is stern to evil.   I remember
A scholar of the Sophists came one day
To teach the people ; a mere youth, but learned,
And learnedly he discoursed of destiny
And learnedly scoffed the Gods.   Antenor paused,

And questioned him : " What wares hast thou for
    sale ? "
" True wisdom, sire." — Whence purchased? whence
    obtained ? "
" Where all men purchase wisdom, in the schools
Of Athens."   Hast thou seen men suffer ? "   " Nay."
" And hast thou known a beautiful woman ? "   " Nay."
" And hast thou faced death ? "   " Nay."
                        Antenor passed.
His silence was like scorn.
    GLAUKA.   My flowers, lady,
Plead to me for the liquor that they love,
And every basin trickles at the brim.
    LUCIUS.   Flowers !   Wrought drops of purest love-
    liness,
So full of silent utterance, like eyes :
Some tender, proud, shy, sad, gay, passionate.
O, beauty is the blossom and the crown
Of everything.   One flower on a vine
Becomes the centre of the world to me.
    GLAUKA.   If yonder nameless bell is opening,
Then it is close on the meridian hour.
At night, or when the rains refresh the hues

And perfumes of the garden, he pouts up
His purple lips.
    Lucius. Thanks for the garland, Glauka.

Glauka sprinkles the flowers in the vases and beds
    near by.

    Adelia. So now thy casque is wreathèd with a
    crown
Fair as thine own Olympian laurel prize.
How swiftly flow the years since thou returnedst,
A victor, from the games !
    Lucius. Yet still thy days
Are those of the young rose when every morn
Unfolds new petals in her riping prime.
Yet how time flows ! It seems a mighty age,
All-thronged with annals of momentous deeds,
Since when my bark, — now fierce-arrayed for war, —
Flew o'er the foamy straits, far out to sea,
Towards Ithaca and the mantled Elian shores.
The picture rises in my memory
When, through Alpheuis's banks in shallops rowing,
We came upon the middle of the games.
Fleet runners, like a herd of startled deer,

Coursed down the track, and supple wrestlers strained,
And chariots clattered in the elliptic ring.
While, high-embanked on stony tiers around,
Reclined the glory and the pride of Greece,
Numberless as the trees that overlay
The flanks of some steep mountain.
                                        Pedestalled
In universal gaze, the reverend bards,
Lyre-laden, sat and mused.   My rivals these,
Who stared at me, the stranger and the boy.
And when my hour was come, — my lyre well clasped,
My fingers in the chords, — I rose, abashed.
The plain of Elis vanished like a dream.
I seemed to see my home ; I seemed to hear
Faint herd-bells of the hills, as when, a boy,
I climbed the mighty Aetna, from the base
Up ladder-vines to some vale-towering peak
That overlooked the sea.   Far southward lay
The undulous fields of Sicily in sight,
Flushed with a flowery haze, red as the stream   -
Ambrosial of thy rose-enamelled cheek, —
Thus flowed my thoughts to thee.   Just then the voice
Of Aeschylus, the minstrel blind, the judge,

Broke on my visions with the subject —
         " Love !
Begin ! " he said.
         I sang the tale eterne
Of two fair souls in youth's gold summer of life,
Who, sauntering through the woodlands arm in arm,
Sink to a seat beneath some shady arbor
Delightful, where the blushing girl first hears
The passionate youth's avowal. Sweet the words
I chose, and pure, and simple, — while my lyre
Breathed murmurous accord, now swelling loud
As with the tender boy's entreaty, now
Expiring softly, like the maiden's sigh.
Singing, my soul waxed wilder. I had risen
To the last outburst of triumphant joy, —
When, lo ! my lyre-strings parted.
         Shattered, dumb,
They lay beneath my fingers. But I cried
Undaunted, "Give me a larger lyre, one meet
To bear the burden of strong ecstasy !
Give me the voice of youths who chant together
With mutual joy, and hearts all tuned in one,
In praise of love — for what is youth but love ?

Give me the tones of that supernal hymn
The blest souls, clustered in Elysian fields,
And fair Pierian groups, Olympian choirs,
Strewn o'er the luminous floor of heaven, pour forth,
Mingled with sweetness of all things that sing,
Of groves, of streams, of winds, of gliding spheres,
Audible to the Gods, or shapes whose veins
Hold ichor, or the rapt, transported bard,
Whose soul, of elemental fires compound,
Hears harmonies divine.   Or, higher still,
Give me the voice of Zeus when by the side
Of Herē he reclines, and through the halls
Of heaven his spoken thunder rings aloud,
Melodious with love.   Such instrument
The mighty passion needs.   A man-made lyre
Breaks with its powerful sweetness."
The echoes died away, and then I knew
That Sicily had won the crown.

ADELIA.   Wear this,
A fairer garland, by as much as love
In life excelleth love in poesy.
But, Glauka, how thou tremblest ! and bright tears
Stand on thy lashes.

GLAUKA.   Something in the tale
Touched me, my lady.

LUCIUS.   Girl, what shade is that
Dwells ever on thy forehead? Is it a pining
For the Euboean home? Or memory
Of one that once smiled on thee in the grove?

ADELIA.   She keeps her story secret from us
    still,
But I am sure 'tis sad. Perhaps red War
Knocked at her city's gate, and, rudely welcomed,
Tore those she loved away. —

LUCIUS (*starting up*).   Banish the fear!
Hope breaks on leaguered Syracuse. The foe
Grow weary, bruising their huge strength in vain
Against our rocky forts. At Camerina
The Spartan lord, Gylippus, waits his chance
To steal through their engirding walls. To-day
The famous Carthaginian general, Barca,
Holds parley with the Senate. With such aid,
(Though more the Spartan valor than the wealth
Of alien, barbarous, and traitor Carthage,)
Our city shall be free. Now task thy arms
To lift my heavy lance.

ADELIA.   So soon, my love?
LUCIUS.   The minutes shrink to seconds by thy side.
But I must seek Antenor.   So farewell,
Until the sun hath risen again.
ADELIA.   Farewell!

They embrace and part.

SCENE II.

The market place.   People flock to and fro.

1ST CITIZEN.   From Carthage?
2ND CITIZEN.   Heaven be praised!   The city's saved.
3RD CITIZEN.   Saved? Does the lion rescue the gazelle
Out of the tiger's clutch?
2ND CITIZEN.   Hath he a force
Attending him?
3RD CITIZEN.   One comrade only.
2ND CITIZEN.   More
Could scarce approach the city unperceived.
3RD CITIZEN.   But if the Senate yields his terms, his
         fleet,
Now moored at Gela, will attack the foe.

For mine own part I think this is a question
Should come before the Assembly of the People.
   4TH CITIZEN. Who's seen the Carthaginian, noble
      Barca?
Hither he makes his way. A mighty form,
Enwrapped in the fantastic Moorish robes, —
Dark, curling locks, and beard like King Darius',
A purple-black, inwoven with threads of gold,
And odorous as a garden.
   3RD CITIZEN.   Luxury
Upon a soldier?
   4TH CITIZEN.   Aye, a famous soldier.
Hush! here he comes.

Enter Barca and Salander with a Syracusan escort.

SALANDER (*to Barca*). The Athenian general,
Nicias, is wasted, and his troops' fresh valor
Departed with defeat.
   BARCA.   It must be so,
Though it were better otherwise. What more?
   SALANDER. From Hellas, far away, the message
      comes
King Agis, on the heights of Decelēa,

Pins Mother Athens' arms, and she must leave
Her army here unsuccored.

BARCA.   One more cause
To side with Syracuse.

Aloud, to the children following them.

                              Come, pretty boy!
Could men engender such a face, Salander?
Two meeting Beauties, essences of air,
A rosy day, when summer was benign,
Being opposite and mutual-fashioned, mingled
In flowery meadows, where the one became
The other, and the other became thee.
Good men of Syracuse, how blest are ye
In your fair children!   Such are never seen
At Carthage in the purest Tyrian strain,
So golden-sunny.   And blessèd in your land,
These soft Sicilian meadows, with mild flocks,
Sweet vegetation, and the tribes of men
Gentle amid the shower of gentleness.
I come from Tunis and the wasted desert,
Accursed of Heaven, where the swarming sands
Close over caravans ; where monster beasts,

Indocile, war on man, and giant trees,
The banyan and the baobab, spread forth
Their axe-defying limbs like groves ; where streams
Through the gnarled forests rolling, disappear
Whither men dare not follow, lost o'er falls
In dark and steaming caverns ; where hot fires
Aye drizzle from the twisting wheels of Day,
And singe the earth and char the face of man.

2ND CITIZEN.   I had as lief be dead in Tartarus
As live in such a country.

CAPTAIN OF ESCORT.   This way, lord.

BARCA.   Ay, let us hasten.

He sets down the child.

CAPTAIN OF ESCORT.   To Antenor's house,
The great High-Priest, our foremost senator.

The people make way.

Scene III.

A room.   The High-Priest and Lucius.

Lucius.   Two things I fain would speak of, reverend
    sire.
This Carthaginian — will the Senators
Accept alliance with him? or is it meet
A question of so grave and general import
Should come before the Assembly?
    Antenor.   We accepted
In name of Syracuse, on terms of 'vantage,
The friendship of Carthago.   Noble Barca
Despatches word to-morrow to his fleet
To muster off Plemmyrium.
    Lucius.   Hath this plan
Thine own approval?
    Antenor.   I proposed the league.
Lord Barca is my guest and dwells with me
Within my mansion-house on Achradina,
Hard by the garden where I shroud from war
My daughter.   Such seemed hospitality
Fitting so famed a guest, and one whose worth
Is infinite to Syracuse.

Lucius.   Forgive me.
For, truly, I revere even as a son
Thy reverend counsels, and believe them truest,
Under the wisdom of the Gods, that men
Devise.   Yet in the judgment of a man
Lesser than thou, thou dost, thou hast done wrong.
The breath of liberty begins to scent
The very winds about us.   I have seen
Our boastful soldiery upon the walls
Tie scrolls upon their arrows, and shoot taunts,
Keener than gashes, at the weary foe.
So near is victory.   Yet underneath
A placid-seeming stream, sharp ears detect
Low murmurs, where the sunken boulders lie.
Two such disturb the current of our life :
First, famine ; secondly, the tyranny
Of your too secret Senate.
     Antenor.   Thus we toil
For Syracuse, and thus doth Syracuse
Requite us !
     Lucius.   The Assembly has not met
This twelvemonth.   At the outset of the siege,
Perplexed by danger, all men looked to you,

Revered your measures, and obeyed you. Now —
Far be it from me to shelter insolence! —
But you misuse the power occasion gave you;
The people are estranged, and if aught ill
Should follow this alliance, I should fear —

 ANTENOR. What?

 LUCIUS.   Mutiny!

 ANTENOR.   Do such rebellious thoughts
Enter their thankless hearts?

 LUCIUS.   The other counsel.
This morning in the market-place, I saw
The priestesses of Aphrodite pass,
With Lais at their head. Softly they wound
Their way towards Achradina, on whose heights
The temple of their revelries doth stand.
Close-veiled all marched, but Lais. She loose-clad;
And to the shoulder her soft-marble arm
Hung bare, and white as snow. No vestal fire
Had it upraised, but it was moulded smooth
For warm caresses and for blandishment.
A hush came o'er the people. Glance met glance.
Then rose a murmur, which when they were passed
Rang forth an execration. " Hast thou heard,"

One cried, " of shades that steal from Lethe lake,
With hideous lamps that throw a jet-black flame,
Dispersing the fair light, and casting gloom
Of hell-fire on the day? oh, these are they."
They cursed the passing women, and the temple,
And cursed the revelries that, two nights hence, —
The yearly night of the Aphrodisia, —
(Unholy pieties, if men speak true),
Are celebrate.   Some say the air is charmed
In one wide circle round the region ; birds
Avoid it as polluted, screaming fear.
Thus fear and hate are in the people's hearts,
Which thou canst turn to love, with one soft word.
Send back these priestesses, collected hither
From who knows what dark dens of shame, Cotytto's
Own priestesses impure !
  ANTENOR.   Dost thou advise me ?
And this advise ?   O recreance of men !
How soon the heart forgets the holy fear
Learned on the pious mother's knee, the prayer
Once printed on the lips, the suppliance
Unto the gracious Gods !
  LUCIUS.   Not pieties they blame, but deeds of night.

Antenor.   They honor Aphrodite, Queen of Heaven.

Lucius.   Not Artemis and Aphrodite, too?

Antenor.   They honor both, the mother and the
    maid.

Lucius.   Words, words.   The rites are impious.
    Sire, forgive

My flaming speech, — my message must be said.

Gold, too, in hoards, they cry, lies treasured there.

An altar in the inmost of the fane

Drinks showers more prodigal than Danae's

From shrine-enamored matrons.   Vases, gems,

All idly deck its chambers, and rich jars,

Filled with a fire that burneth to our shame,

Or brimmed with unguents for the milky limbs

Unclean of Lais' sisters.   We are poor.

The people cry for bread, and gold to buy

The bread from friendly Gela.   Seize the temple!

Antenor.   Impious youth!

Lucius.   Ay, seize the fane, they cry.

Melt down the ewers and put the cleansing stamp

Of Syracuse's mint on gold, pollute

With orgies.

Antenor.   O thou mistress of the skies!

Thou mother of the miracle that joins
Woman with man in marriage, and creates
New men arising while the old descend,
Like waves that toss continuous on at sea,
Turn not thy wrath upon these fools that scorn
Thine oracle, thy priestesses, thy fane !
Youth, go ! We have no ears for calumny.
No hand shall stay the rites of Aphrodite.
No gold shall leave her altar, save by theft
Most sacrilegious.

    Lucius.   Sire, the people starve.

    Antenor. Too well I know the woe that over-
      hangs us.

Could I appease their hunger with my flesh,
Or cool their thirst with the red stream of blood
That fills my heart, think'st thou I would not give
    them ?

    Lucius. Far lesser is the sacrifice they ask.

    Antenor. Nay, who dares brave the anger of the
      Gods,

The mystic monarchs, whose imperative
Dumb elements obey, and only man
Demurreth, to his woe. Did they with voice

Of awe, as they of old in sacred story
Called Agamemnon, the Argolian king,
Call *me* to lead my daughter to the shrine,
And quench with these old hands my star of love,
My soul's delight, my glory, my Adelia —
    Lucius.   O God!
    Antenor.   I would obey their high commandment.
    Lucius.   But think, my lord, —
    Antenor.   Son, I have spoken.   Go!

Act Second.

SCENE I.

Next morning. The market place. Wailing of women and uproar of men. A group of sailors, one of whom is speaking.

SAILOR. We three were cruising in the bay last
  night.
With dawn the wind blew fresher, and we saw
Among the white-caps, half a league away,
A hundred war-ships, with the Attic ensign
Fluttering at the mast.   The bugles blew
A welcome from the shore, and Charon cried
" Demosthenes is come!   Home with the news!"
But one proud galley, fleeter than the rest,
Came towards us like the wind.   We tacked to meet
  her.
Her prong went through poor Captain Andros' sloop.
Two others tangled Charon in between them,
And twenty chased me home.

WOMEN.   Wo! Wo! Wo! Wo!
Wo! Wo! to Syracuse.

CITIZENS.   The city's lost! —
O, for Gylippus with the help from Sparta! —
Too late! too late! —

     Call the Assembly! —

           Ay,
Call the Assembly!

     Can they make us men? —
And ships? —

    And bread to save us from the famine?

WOMEN. Wo! Wo! Wo! Wo! Wo! Wo!
 to Syracuse.

A CITIZEN. Who was it spoke of famine? I'd not
 heard
The island was grown barren. Are not stalks
Still green, and fruit still red, in Sicily?

CITIZENS. Thou mock'st us, Citizen Petros. Well
 thou knowest
All our allies are poorer than ourselves,
And we've no gold to purchase from the rest.

CITIZEN PETROS.   You *have* gold.

CITIZENS.   Where?

CITIZEN PETROS.   In Aphrodite's temple.
CITIZENS. Oh!

Murmurs.

CITIZEN PETROS. Shrink not, friends! 'Tis yours.
     Now, while the way
Lies open through the fort, where Captain Lucius
Holds Nicias' walls asunder, — gaping jaws,
All-fain to close on hapless Syracuse ! —
Rifle the fane! Send merchants to the marts
Of Camerina, shepherds to range for flocks
The inland pastures.   There is treasure there
Would purchase a month's life for Syracuse.
Give us but bread, and with the men and ships
We have, we'll guard the city till Gylippus
Arrives from Lacedaemon.
     CITIZENS.   Seize the temple !
Prevent the Aphrodisia !
                         Down with Lais !
Down with the Senate !

Enter Lucius.

LUCIUS.   Friends, I thought I heard
The voice of mutiny.   What has befallen ?

Women in tears, with children clinging round them,
And all your faces cheerless?

CITIZEN PETROS.   Bitter tidings!
Demosthenes is anchored at Plemmyrium
With seventy triremes.

LUCIUS.   O thou God of Justice,
How have we sinned that thou, even at the hour
When hope was rosiest, shouldst heap the odds
Against us to so mountainous a volume?

WOMEN. Wo! Wo! Wo! Wo! Wo! Wo! to
      Syracuse.

LUCIUS.   What can I do to still your anguish?   Tell
      me,
And I will do it.

CITIZENS.   Call the Assembly! —
Prevent the midnight revels! —

                         Seize the treasure!
The treasure, or we yield.

LUCIUS.   Surely, you are
No Syracusans, but base foreigners.
Did they outnumber us, as waves the rock,
Bid them defiance, like our ancestors,
When Xerxes posted his imperial seal

Upon Thessalian Athos, and the hordes
Hung over little Hellas like a cloud.

    CITIZEN PETROS.   O, thou and I, Lord Lucius, we
        are men,
And we could bear the fast. But what of these,
Our nursing mothers, children, agèd ones,
All hollow-cheeked with hunger? This because
The feeble Senate rules us! This because
One agèd priest invokes the curse of God
On them who stir his treasure! Fond Antenor!
Not blessings, but rude wrath are Heaven's response
For these, our shameful Aphrodisia,
Writ in no Hellene calendar, but drawn
From the luxurious Orient.

    LUCIUS.   Good friends,
What's hunger, weighed with plunder, rapine, chains,
And endless slavery in the mines of Laurium?
Talk not of yielding, then. Think not the word.
It is impossible. But if you will —
You are the people — muster! congregate!
Run hither, thither, bid each citizen,
Captain, or scribe, ye meet upon your way,
Gather at the Assembly-House : and there

Take ye good counsel.   For what ye do there
Is law for Syracuse.

    Citizen Petros.   And for the Senate.

    Citizens.   The Assembly ! —

                The Assembly ! —

                    The Assembly !

Demosthenes is come ! —

           Call the Assembly !

Scene II.

Antenor's House.   Barca and Salander.

    Barca.   My forehead aches with subtleties.   Three
      plans
Have perished in the germ within an hour,
But one is bourgeoning.   Just now it bore
A flower, the fairest organ of the herb,
The cradle of the fruit. — Demosthenes
Is come.

    Salander.   Thou echoest the people's cry,
But not their anguished accent : for thy tone
Seems joyous.

BARCA.   Can the city stand before him?

SALANDER.   He is a famous general.

BARCA.   If we locked
Our strength with his, how long could Syracuse
Withstand our double army?

SALANDER.   But the walls
Of Syracuse are round us.   To depart
At such a moment would proclaim us spies,
Not legates; and as such, if I mistake not,
We should be treated by the Syracusans.

BARCA.   In my first dream of conquest, these slight
        isles
Appeared an easy prey.   I thought to gird
All Sicily with fleets, and at her ports
Take toll of her ripe harvests.   Then I saw
On either hand Illyria, Italy,
Greece, Gallia to the rocks of Hercules,
And all the nations of the Mediterranean,
Enrich our boundless empire.   Every town
Upon a river's mouth, and every ship
That ploughed the bosom of this inland ocean
Carthage should own; and, like a mightier sea,
O'erflow its shores and thunder at the base

Of the northern Alps, that loom impregnable
And fend us from the snows.   For this I lured
Vain Athens on to storm this puissant city,
And would have lent her aid, but Nicias,
The weakling, courted failure, and I donned
The mask of friendship to win entrance here
Into the heart of Syracuse.   Now fortune
Changes her smile, and I throw off the mask.
We must escape to the Athenians.

    SALANDER.   Escape?   But how? and when?

    BARCA.   To-morrow midnight,
It is the season of the Aphrodisia,
Which these Greeks hate : and now, by famine crazed,
And fear, and hatred of the haughty Senate,
They swear they will prevent them ; while my host,
Impracticable priest, resists their clamor,
And swears they shall be held.   Out of this feud
I'll draw the clash of steel, whence shall leap forth
A spark which shall cosuume the hated temple,
And Syracuse beside.

    SALANDER.   How, master ?

    BARCA.   Listen.
Demosthenes, that night, forewarned in time,

Shall fall upon the embroilèd Syracusans, —
Unarmed, in mutiny, and unsuspecting, —
Scale their sea-wall, and swarm their avenues
With irresistible might.

SALANDER.   Hast bribed some Greek
To bear the message to Demosthenes?

BARCA.   Nay, that's a service of a deeper faith
Than gold could buy.   Thou would'st not fear to swim
Across the harbor to the Athenian fleet?

SALANDER.   Fear, master?

BARCA.   Thou wilt bear the message, then.
I stay to hide thy flight, and 'mid the riot
Will easily make way.   But —

                    Hast thou marked
The beauty of Antenor's child, Adelia?
There's music in the name!   Adelia!

SALANDER.   Which?

BARCA.   The taller of the twain, the one whose
        cheeks
Show waves of blushes.   Yea, she must be mine.
Oh, she is luscious as a Lesbian grape,
That drop of unpressed wine.   Yet in her eye
A glance superior, an inborn law,

O'errules my else unbridled love.   I would
She had some trivial fault, some little spot !
Hath she a brother?

    SALANDER.   How should I know, master?

    BARCA.   I would she had!   In him I'd read her
      faults.

Her womanhood mists them over.   O, I rave.
She hath no faults ; she is perfect as the stone
I wear upon my finger.

    SALANDER.   Hast forgot

Poor, dark-eyed Hari ?   She would grieve to hear
How thou dost praise the azure-eyed Adelia.

    BARCA.   Poor Hari !   I am inconstant unto thee.
But why inconstant ?   'Tis no single rose
We love, although a queen ; 'tis but the kind.
For any rose is fair.   From this and that
We smell the delicate odor ; here and there
We pluck one.   So with women as with roses.
'Tis scarce inconstancy.
But mark !   she must be mine.

    SALANDER.   Speak, master, on.
I've served thee twenty years, and never seen
Such knots of tangled danger.

BARCA.   We must seize
The maiden on that night.
    SALANDER.   How slip the guard ?
How reach the shore ?
    BARCA.   If but the light of heaven
Is veiled, how far can man's poor torches pierce
Earth's shadow ?   Hast thou never seen by night
A sleeping city on a shore afar,
How like mere sparks the lights gleamed, thinly scat-
       tered
Amid the darksome mass ?   Each bank of gloom
Housed felons and their deeds.   So shall the night
Befriend *us*.   But I must be expeditious.
Upon this tablet I will brand the message,
Which slip beneath the sole-piece of thy sandal ;
Then thong it tightly.   Plunge, and thou'rt away,
While I go brew a charm of slumb'rous herbs
To drug the fair Adelia.   'Mid the uproar,
With her, embalmed in poison-sleep, — a burden
That I could lift o'er Atlas' ridge, I think, —
I'll reach the shore, and keep in hiding there
Till ye arrive.   That I may know thee sooner,
Hang up a red light in thy galley.   Hush !

Antenor comes — and bid Demosthenes
Be prompt ! — This was the flower of my plan,
That cradles the blest fruit.

Scene III.

A hall.   The fifty captains of Syracuse.

Lucius.   Age against age,
Sloth against laggard caution, feeble will
Against irresolution and delay,
Such, brothers, is the story of this siege
While Nicias and our Senate faced each other.
But now the young Demosthenes arrives,
Ever-victorious, in whose armament
I see the doom of Syracuse, if we,
The city's captains, skilled and bold in war,
Match not our might with his, — youth against youth,
Swift counsel 'gainst swift counsel, and hard blows
Against hard blows.
        1st Captain.   Why, I have been in sieges
Where every face was cheerful as a band
Of maidens on a holiday.   For each

Had wrought and riveted upon his soul
The viewless, but invulnerable armor
Of adamantine courage.   But look round,
And see the tear-wet faces, telling tales
Of trembling hearts.   Are then our people cowards?
By Mars!   I do not brag, but there are none
Braver in all the world ; and if some scourge
Swept off our army in a night, our wives
Would man the empty walls and fight the foe.
But there's one foe strikes foul, and few so brave
As not to fear him, — Famine!   Woe the word!
This have our guilty Senate drawn upon us
By their imprudent spendings, and now stand
Too witless to relieve the misery
Their witlessness has caused.

    Lucius.   Good friend, we owe
A reverence to white hairs.   Whate'er our acts,
Still let our words be kind.

    1st Captain.   What owe we then
Unto the people, whose Assembly, held
This very hour, commissions us with power
Supreme, to rule the city?   At my post
My soldiers are awaiting me.   I ask

Some means to check the midnight revelries,
Orgies and dances and demoniac laughter,
That else will mock in silence of the night
Upon yon hill the misery of the city.

   2ND CAPTAIN. The wealthiest shrine in Sicily.
     What shame
To put this gold to evil use, which, turned
To good, would prove so potent! Hear my plan.
To-morrow night let's march to Achradina,
Disperse the priestesses, and seize the treasure,
Then burn the cursed pollution to the ground!

   CAPTAINS. Well counselled! We approve!

   2ND CAPTAIN.   Vague whispers passed
Will reassure the people all is well.

   CAPTAINS. Ay, we approve!

   2ND CAPTAIN.   Antenor must not know,
Nor any Senator. When all is done,
Then let them fume in vain.

   CAPTAINS.   Ay, we approve!

   LUCIUS. Brothers, I beg you think me not behind
In hatred of the revels, nor in wish
To gain the needed treasure for the people.
And yet, beware of haste. The sculptor moulds

No statue from the snow-banks in the fields,
Though of a more than Parian tissue, pure
And pliant to the skill of supple fingers.
Better the marble block that but with toil
And sweat gives shape, cold, everlasting shape
To burning thoughts. Better the slow-wrought counsel!
Something in the proposal I approve,
Something I fear. I love the aim ; I fear
The haste, the violence, the secrecy.

   1st Captain. One voice of mild dissuasion. Thou
      hast cause
To love Antenor, Lucius. It is meet
To honor the High-Priest. But, grieve who will,
This treasure must be ours, — the revels checked, —
Ay, and the temple burned. If openly
We cry our purpose forth — thou know'st Antenor,
The rocky will, from which rebound alike
Entreaty and command.

   Lucius.   Be it not said
By him who writes our tale in years to come,
Twining a garland of sweet poesy
Around my lance of war, that even the voice
Of love had power against the voice of duty,

Or that I, fearing to grieve my lord Antenor,
Wronged all the Syracusans.   I approve.
    1st Captain.   Seal the deliberation with an oath.
By father Zeus, the king of Gods and men,
By Styx' black stream, the oath unutterable,
By all things sacred, mortal and immortal,
We set the seal of silence on our lips.
    All.   We set the seal of silence on our lips.

Scene IV.

Antenor's House.   Barca and Antenor.

    Antenor.   Name me the godless rebels!
    Barca.   For the names —
My comrade overheard the plot, — Salander,
A worthy soldier, — at to-morrow midnight
They were to march and burn some temple, — which,
I know not, — seize its treasures, and disperse
The priestesses assembled.   Being a stranger,
Unskilled in Greek, my comrade missed the names.
I, fearing treason, which forever basks
In secrecy, and eager to give earnest

Of my devotion, which has hitherto
Lived only in professions, brought the tale,
To thee, most reverend in authority —
    ANTENOR. I reverend! Nay, I am the meanest
      slave.
Dost thou not see my priestly office mocked,
Myself a scorn for strangers, violent hands
Constraining me to do their evil will?
O faithless generation! Do ye think
No judging eye beholds ye through the dark?
And fear ye not His thunderbolt, the missile
No mortal speed can shun, no shield can ward?
It smites the haughty eagle as he soars,
Strong-winged, above the peaks, amid the storm ;
Down through the heavens the zigzag lightning bursts,
And cleaves him, and he falls. So ye shall fall.
    BARCA. My sword is thine. Enroll me in the band
Thou marshall'st to chastise them.
    ANTENOR.   Generous stranger,
Thy singular devotion pierces me.
I would I knew the names. Nay, sheathe thy sword.
Leave me to intercept the deed of shame ;
It is beneath thine office. In thy name,

O powerful Aphrodite, in the name
Of Syracuse, lest vengeance overtake
This impious crime, I'll summon to my side
The faithful and the good.   I thank thy zeal,
Lord Barca.   Would I knew the names.   My task
Were easier.

    BARCA.   Poor priest! It needs no craft
To work on thee.   Now for Demosthenes.

SCENE V.

*A bower in the secluded garden.   Twilight.   Lucius
and Adelia.*

˙ADELIA.

Now day departeth like a fading smile
That lingers on the lips of sea and heaven ;
And men float dreamward to the blessed isle
Of slumber, o'er a drowsy ocean driven
By night, the beauteous and the mourning mother.
Now one by one the vesper stars aloft
Steal through the gathering gloom ; and hush! oh,
    hush!

For here and there and all about us, soft,
Cool water-music bubbles, like the gush
Of garden springs that sing to one another.

Lucius.

If to be dead were but to dwell in pleasance
Amid the glories of yon sunset sky,
Hanging above the earth, a God-like presence,
High in the west, were it not sweet to die?
O fiery radiance, what art thou, say?
Thy hues outrival Iris, and shame Flora,
When, breaking early buds o'er hill and hollow,
She leadeth through the lands the month of May!
Art thou a vision of the young Aurora,
That visitest the slumbers of Apollo?

Adelia.

Whether the final harmony is death,
And all this life melts out in subtle fusion
With yon Sky-Presence, at surcease of breath, —
Reunion with the world, sweet dissolution,
As of a dew-drop in the morning air;
Whether our souls live forward to some flower

Of soul-perfection, 'mid a spirit host,
Aye hung like incense-clouds before a Power
Of majesty divine ; Oh, who can boast
To know the answer of that question fair ?

Lucius.

I would not live where there is no communion
With thee, O lordly Nature, no full sight
Of all thy beauteous parts, in sweetest union,
My love, my meditation, my delight.
In thee the waters and the woods abide ;
In thee the bough-bird sings, in summer's van ;
This is thy changeful sky, now seamed with levin,
Now blue and calm ; on thee, as on a bride
The beautiful poet, young and shy of man,
Presses his burning heart, and murmurs " Heaven ! "

Adelia.

He loves, and listens for the warm response,
Love's sweetness ; but the siren's breast is hollow,
Empty of love.   The forests and the fonts
Regard him not, and when he fain would follow
The sweet, wild doe, she, with misgiving eyes,

Flees farther in the glade. Cold is the light,
Cold the unspeakable, eye-delighting glow
That filleth heaven when day is born or dies.
Nay, poet shy of man, man will requite
Thy love with love cold Nature cannot know.

LUCIUS.

Thy soul is learnèd in the lore of love.
Teach me the wisdom in thy bosom chambered.
Yea, to be prized all other things above,
Smiled on, endeared, nay, but to be remembered
Upon that other shore of Death's dead stream,
By one pure maiden here, to wed two hearts
Like thine and mine, is rapture deeper, higher,
Than contemplation, or the poet's dream,
Or tinselled treasure of the whole world's marts.
'Tis the fruition of all soul's desire.

ADELIA.

Look, love, without! How yon gold dial shines,
Whose needle's shadow marks the moving hour.
And shafts of splendor pierce the lacing vines
That, thick-embranching, darken all the bower.

The moon hath risen by stealth to overhear us,
And night's black garb is silvered with a hue
Not on the rainbow palette of the day.
Look, where with phosphoral path a meteor flew ;
But ere thou turnest it hath waned away
Behind yon bank of cloud that floateth near us.

LUCIUS.

Hast ever marked, amid the golden signs,
A vague-felt shimmer of unseen starlight playing
Behind the globèd orbs ?   My soul divines
A myriad stars, imbedding and inlaying
Invisible spheres, yet to be seen of men.
Thus oft are thoughts foreshadowed by the soul,
Beyond the very verge of mortal sight,
Which Time, unrolling the unending scroll
Of truth, reads ages after.   Hark ! the night
Is riven by a voice — again ! — again !

Glauka's voice is heard afar, singing.

ARIADNE.

I make my pillow
A mossy stone,

Sleeping alone
Under the willow,
Under the weeping tree.
The nightingale
Mocks in my ear,
Singing so near
Out of the vale,
"Sweet is my life to me!
Sweet is my life to me!"

My home was a palace,
And hers a bough,
But now, ah, now!
She drinks a chalice
Of rapture and I of rue.
No fair-faced lover
Led her away,
And then one day
Sailed off, false rover,
Bidding her never adieu ;
Bidding me never adieu.

Voices of flowers sing softly :

Hark ! hark ! a nightingale is in the garden ;
Or one of the orioles that linger long
In Sicily's lovely woodlands.   Pardon, pardon,
'Tis Philomel's own inarticulate song,
Lip-broken into words.   Adieu!   Adieu!
How softly in the air the echoes float!
While in yon leafy bower two lovers true,
Severing with tears, repeat the plaintive note.
Adieu!   all things are parting.   Let us flowers,
Rose, lily, dahlia, heliotrope, camellia, —
List to the lovely naming of our choir, —
Answer Adieu!   Adieu!   fair daylight hours ;
Adieu!   bright stars ; Adieu!   brown bird of fire ;
Adieu!   sweet lovers, Lucius and Adelia.

Act Third.

SCENE I.

A moonlight night. The Temple of Aphrodite. On a sloping bank that leads down from the temple, youths recline with lyres. Fountains play at the sides. In front, on a level lawn, maidens dance. Slow music, gradually quickening.

MAIDENS.

While men seek slumber and the tired flocks rest,
And o'er their path in heaven's eternal arch
The eastern stars are floating to the west,
    The moon o'erhangs the sea ;
We, Aphrodite's nymphs, in garb of snow,
With hallowed dances round her temple march,
Chanting the happy choruses that flow
    From joyous ecstasie.

Come, bloomy maid, come join our merry bands,
And leave the drowsy virgins to their dreams,
Roam up with us the sloping mountain lands
    Where winds blow wild and cool ;
Oft loitering on the banks to bathe thy locks
In the delicious waters of the streams ;
Or, if in any basin of the rocks
    They pour a crystal pool,

All screened in shrubs, and brinked with flowers of
    gold,
Wherein, perchance, the naked naiad swims,
There slip the knots and girdles that enfold
    Thy Cytherean bloom,
And in the unrippled water-mirror mark
The lily beauty of thy spotless limbs,
That gleam like marble in the dewy dark
    And all the lake illume.

YOUTHS.

Come, youth, leave strife and fierce alarms,
The clangor of steel and the pain of blows,

And repose, like Mars, in the soft, warm arms
    Of thy Venus, from the war.
Her lips say "Away," but her eyes say "Come!"
And her cheeks outvie the superb wild rose,
And her tresses the fleece of Elysium
    That the Argo voyaged for.

Come, follow the maids who day and night
Heed but the sense and the longing of joy
That fills man's blood with a wild delight,
    Veining him as with fire.
Come, take thy part in the ring-round whirl,
On thy right hand Eros, the lovely boy,
On thy left a red-lipped, laughing girl,
    All dancing to my lyre.

Come where the nightingale learned to sing,
From Aleale, sweeter than she,
Whom we chase through the valleys, abloom with spring,
    But still she escapes afar.
For when we are nearest, away! away!
She outruns Atalanta over the lea,
And sings in her flight like a lark at day
    Taking wing for the morning star.

Lais.

When Aphrodite rose from the foam
'Mid shining drops that clung in showers —

*The temple bursts into flame. The fifty captains appear
on its steps.*

Lucius.   Away, foul women! Thou, with raven
  hair
That flecks thy snowy shoulders, — Fallen Lais!
I would mine eye were solid fire to brand
Red shame upon thy forehead, and bring back
The blush of maidenhood that dyed thy cheeks,
When, still a smiling girl, thou dwelt at home
Among thy people, wayward but beloved.
What do ye here on this unhappy night,
When every woman's bed in Syracuse
Should be bedewed with tears, bidding this hill
Shake with the light-foot dances till it rocks
The citizen from his troubled sleep below?
He wakes and hears, then sleeps again and dreams
The Furies ride the night winds, trumpeting
Wild, demon laughter o'er the hapless city.

*He comes forward. The High-Priest and a guard rush
in, and surround the captains and the dancers.*

ANTENOR.   Lucius!—Must I believe
Mine eyes and not my heart? Thou, whom I loved
Even as a son, because my daughter loved thee,
The daily vision of whose fair young face
Gladdened my heart. For " Now the rust of age
Is in my hair, the winter in my beard,"
Thought I, "soon must my daughter bear her fruit
To greet me ere I die, as springtime buds
Greet withering winter. Noble is the blood
That mingles for their birth. So shall they be
Well-worthy scions of Antenor's line."
Sooner would I have thought mine own right hand
Intrigued against me than that thou would'st do
This cunning deed, at which the vaulted sky
Should burst, and vengeance fall the ancient path,
Straight, swift, from God's own hand.
    LUCIUS.   Most reverend sire,
Are these thy ministers? This midnight orgie
Thy holy festival? Thou canst not know
What lewd and evil follies festered here, —
The wanton motions, dances, satyr-songs

Fouling the lips of maidens.   If these things
Are holy, we blaspheme, with torch and sword
Blaspheme ; though on the eternal calendar
Of Him whose heart is grieved by deeds of shame,
I think such blasphemy would write our names
In glory, not in blame.   And call our deed
Not cunning, though we wear the secret mask
Of night in it.   But for thy sake the deed
Were blazoned forth to daylight, that all men
Might hail it with rejoicing.   Well we feared
The blow we aimed at sin would fall on thee,
Who art the noble shield of things ignoble.
So now thou know'st our purpose was not ill.
I kiss thy robes, — unbend thine iron frown,
And speak a golden blessing on our deed,
Our honorable deed, which brings heart's ease
Unto the Syracuse thou lovest dearly.

    ANTENOR.   Rebuild,
Rebuild yon massy roof, festooned with fires
That shrivel up its marble majesty
To ashes in mine eyes.   Then ask my blessing.
Son, son, I will not curse thee.   Pour, O heavens,
Thy fountains on these fires, that he may live,

If it is just he live. — No answer comes ;
Nought but a fiercer sighing of the flames.
That vault high up the night, and weirdly fling
Wild-leaping shadows o'er us. As when rains
Hiss o'er the tropic seas and whirlwinds lash
The bare, broad back of ocean, on the base
Of some huge cliff the billows, breaking, toss
Huge flakes of foam in air, so rise the waves
Of conflagration o'er the fated fane,
And one by one the pillars bend and fall.
Enough ! bind them and him.

LUCIUS.   What would'st thou do ?
Not bind the fifty captains of the city,
Her nobles and commanders ?

ANTENOR.   By the Gods,
Whose laws outweigh all usages of men,
Both they and thou shall answer on the morrow
Before a meet tribunal for this crime.

LUCIUS. Wreak all thy sacred vengeance on my head,
But I implore thee, stir no bloody feud.
Sheathe up thy sword !

ANTENOR.   Not until every knave
Surrenders.

CAPTAINS.   Insolent priest, beware !

ANTENOR.   Upon them !

The guard attacks the captains.

LUCIUS.   Antenor !   Comrades !

(*A shriek.*)

The moon !

PRIESTESSES.   The moon !

                              The moon !

ANTENOR.   What miracle
Arrests your waving blades ?   How all the air
Grows black as Styx !

*The priestesses prostrate themselves.   The captains
draw back.   The moon is eclipsed.*

VOICES.   The moon !

ANTENOR.   O Artemis !
Dost thou conceal thy pure, pale face aloft
Against the deeds of men, and set the sign
Of God's displeasure, the far-feared eclipse,
Upon the face of heaven ?   Trembling I cast
Mine eyes to thee, and I am cold with fear,
Although my heart is clean.   O what confusion

Must fill the hearts of them who dare profane
God's mysteries, and set their littleness
'Gainst his triumphant grandeur !

Low chant of Priestesses.

Artemis ! Artemis ! shine again,
Hide the frown of thine awful anger ;
Heed the prayer of thy meek adorers,
　　Stricken with fear of thy righteous wrath.
　　While the eyes of wrangling men
Saw but each other, thou, unobservèd,
Stole away to the dark horizon,
　　Leaving the night all black in thy path.
　　Artemis ! Artemis ! shine again.
　　Artemis ! Artemis ! shine again.

A pause.

ANTENOR.　Is not the meaning of the Gods writ plain
Upon the dome of heaven ?
　　LUCIUS.　　　　　Whoe'er they be
That interpose to check this fatal strife,
I thank them.　Comrades, sheathe your swords.

Antenor,
Let them depart, for Syracuse hath need
Of her commanders on the walls to-night.
Bind me, and I will pledge my life for them
To stand with me, and answer on the morrow
The charges thou shalt make.

ANTENOR.   So let it be.
Bitter, oh bitter, is my heart to see
Thee, Lucius, bound, a felon, at my feet.
For what tribunal, though of love and mercy
Impanelled, could adjudge thee innocent?
Thy guilt is clear as sunlight.   With this chain
I set thy doom upon thee.

LUCIUS.   Comrades, sheathe
Your swords, and heed him not.   To-morrow stand
And plead for Lucius, not with angry steel,
But with the voice of reason at the throne
Of Reason's daughter, Justice.

The moon comes out.

PRIESTESSES.   Artemis!

A multitude has gathered.

ANTENOR. Arise, ye servants of the holy **Gods** ;
Arise, good citizens, and let them stoop
In fear, on whom the goddess casts her frown.
For us she smiles, approving what we do.
Arise and join my prayer.

Chant, led by Antenor.

ANTENOR. To the Lórd, Gíver of áll góod, to the
móst Hígh,

CHORUS. To the Lórd, Gíver of áll góod, to the
móst Hígh,

ANTENOR. Be the héarts lífted, the práyers úttered,
the wórks gíven,

CHORUS. Be the héarts lífted, the práyers úttered,
the wórks gíven,

ANTENOR. Of all mén dwélling on éarth únder the
bróad sún !

CHORUS. Of all mén dwélling on éarth únder the
bróad sún !

ANTENOR. Him the vást pówers, enthróned hígh in
the húge Héaven,

CHORUS. Him the vást pówers, enthróned hígh in
the húge Héaven,

ANTENOR. Him the dárk mónarchs whose réalms
líe where the déad líe,

CHORUS. Him the dárk mónarchs whose réalms líe
where the déad líe,

ANTENOR. Him the lóst ónes, the unféaríng, the
foul sín-shód,

CHORUS. Him the lóst ónes, the unféaríng, the foul
sín-shód,

ANTENOR. Him the fáir fólk that on éarth's rím a
life-ráce rún,

CHORUS. Him the fáir fólk that on éarth's rím a life-
ráce rún,

ANTENOR. All obéy, shúnning the dréad wráth of
the Lórd Gód,

CHORUS. All obéy, shúnning the dréad wráth of the
Lórd Gód,

ANTENOR. Of the Lórd Gód, of the Lórd Gód, of
the Lórd Gód,

CHORUS. Of the Lórd Gód, of the Lórd Gód, of the
Lórd Gód.

ANTENOR. When the dárk témpest invádes Héaven,
with its wíde wíngs

CHORUS. When the dárk témpest inwádes Héaven, with its wíde wíngs

ANTENOR. Far outspréad óver the bríght líght of the dáy-stár,

CHORUS. Far outspréad óver the bríght líght of the dáy-stár,

ANTENOR. And the áir glóoms in their bláck sháde, and the séas súrge,

CHORUS. And the áir glóoms in their black shade, and the séas súrge,

ANTENOR. And the sóft hármony, jóy-blówn, that the wínd síngs

CHORUS. And the sóft hármony, jóy-blówn, that the wínd síngs

ANTENOR. Turns to díscórd and the stránge shríeks of the stórm-dírge

CHORUS. Turns to díscórd and the stránge shríeks of the stórm-dírge

ANTENOR. Till the ráinbów on the hílls séts her tíará.

CHORUS. Till the ráinbów on the hílls séts her tíará.

ANTENOR. Then all héarts bów to the dréad wráth of the Lórd Gód,

CHORUS. Then all héarts bów to the dréad wráth of
the Lórd Gód,

ANTENOR. Of the Lórd Gód, of the Lórd Gód, of
the Lórd Gód.

CHORUS. Of the Lórd Gód, of the Lórd Gód, of the
Lórd Gód

SCENE II.

*Out in the harbor. The eclipse. Burning temple in
the distance. Barca in a skiff.*

BARCA. Where were ye, false Athenians? Saw ye
not

My beacon on the heights of Syracuse?

O, had ye answered it, the town were mine,

Adelia mine. — I watched her by the shore.

But chance would have it that my flashing blade

Betrayed me to a guard. By rock and bank

Long I eluded them, until at last

The hue and cry grew louder at my heels.

This chance-found shallop saved me. But I lost

Adelia. She lies slumbering on the beach,
And I am far away. Courage! Are those
The ghostly outlines of a fleet at anchor?
They hang a lantern in the foremost galley.
Friends! — How my voice sounds hollow in the
    night! —
They heard me not. The vessels' sides are lined
With sailors, staring at the double portent,
The burning temple and the hidden moon.
Salander!

A Voice.   Master, is it thou?
Barca.   'Tis I.
Salander.   The Gods be praised, I trembled for
    thy life.

Barca rows near.

Barca.   What keeps ye here?
Salander.   Astarte's darkening.
We put to sea, and just had caught the breeze,
When lo! she masked her light. The augurs cried
It was an evil omen, and Lord Nicias
Bade us return.
Barca.   O magic-ridden fool!

SALANDER.   Methought at first the plan was over-
bold.

BARCA.   My plan was perfect as a crystal sphere
That wizards study for the laws of numbers.
But it is hard to walk through life as men
Are doomed to walk, backward, and shun the rock
Of hazard in our way. — Take me aboard,
And bring me to Demosthenes.

Act Fourth.

Scene I.

On the beach, next morning.   Glauka and Adelia.

ADELIA (*waking*).   O such a dream !   Where am I ?
GLAUKA.   On the beach,
Dear lady.
ADELIA.   Who art thou ?
GLAUKA.   Why, I am Glauka,
Dost thou not know me ?
ADELIA.   So thou art.   At first,
I did not know thee.
GLAUKA.   Pray, what brought thee here
Unto this lonely region of the shore ?
ADELIA.   Here ! — Where ? — Are we in Syracuse ?
GLAUKA.   Why, surely.
Thou know'st the houses and the fields around.
ADELIA.   There is a mist upon mine eyes.   Ah,
     now,

Now I remember.   It was in the garden,
At eventide ; I broidered in my bower
With idle fingers, thinking of my betrothcd,
And smiling at my thoughts.   When lo! I felt
A fume of spices, myrrh, and poppy-juice
And strange aromas floating in the air,
And all so thick compounded that they made
A sickening sweetness, and my breath came heavy,
My eyelids drooped, and I had sunk aswoon,
But two broad, mighty arms embraced me.   "Hush!"
A voice said.   "Have no fear.   I love thee, love thee."
And when I oped my eyes, thou canst not think
Whose burning gaze met mine?

GLAUKA.   Truly, I cannot.

ADELIA.   The Carthaginian, Barca.

GLAUKA.   Wonderful!
O wonderful!

ADELIA.   Mine eyes were sealed in slumber,
Yet still some faint sense in me was astir
Of being borne upon the wind, on, on,
As if I were a bird.   I heard the plash
Of waves, and murmur of the sea ; then shouts
Pursuing, and the mighty arms embraced

Me closer, and we flew with fiercer speed.
Until at last I felt myself laid down
As lightly as a mother lays her babe
Upon its downy cradle. Night and silence
Around me, close to my ear the dashing waves.
I slept, — and when I woke just now 'twas lightsome.
  GLAUKA. Yes, it is morning, love. The night is
    over.
O such a fearful night! I tossed and tossed
Upon my bed, and never slept a wink,
So full of uproar was the city. Dawn
Awoke me, palely gazing through my curtains,
And I arose. Attired, I cast a glance
Into thy chamber. Thou wast gone, thy couch
Unpressed. I called thee, softly as I could,
Not to awake thy father in the house.
For still I thought thou hadst but slept o'ernight
In some still corner of the garden. Nay,
Thy bower was empty. Only the dawn-choir
Of thrushes answered me. Bewildered then
I passed without the gate. What drew my steps
Down toward the beach, I know not. On this brink
I found thee, slumbering, like an ocean-maid

High-stranded by the tide. I touched and kissed
And rocked thee, all in vain. The wings of sleep
Were locked above thy brow, thy marble brow,
And as I watched thee, lo! the rising sun
Shone warmer, and the breeze 'gan gently chafe
Thy cheeks to their own bloom. Thy bosom sighed,
Thy lips 'gan move, murmuring "Such a dream!"

ADELIA. A wondrous story! Nay, dear, I am
 strong.
Were it not best go tell my father of it?

GLAUKA. Love, thou art faint and dizzy.

ADELIA.   I am sure
'Twas Barca. Canst thou think why he should wish
To bring me hither, Glauka?

GLAUKA.   Nay, I cannot.
But we must tell thy father. Canst thou walk
Along the beach?

ADELIA.   There is a cottage, yonder.
The people seem astir.

GLAUKA.   This way, Adelia.
It is the smoother path.

Scene II.

The Senate-House, an open theatre. The Senate sit-
ting as tribunal. The High-Priest as accuser;
Lucius and the captains as accused. The urn of
Pardon and the urn of Death. Populace. Ruins
of temple visible on the hill.

Antenor. No more, out on the sea, rounding the
    cape
Pachynus, shall the foreign mariner,
Whence'er the beauteous crest of Syracuse
Looms in the northern horizon, enthroned
Upon its rocky mountain, say "There stands
Some old, illustrious capital, beloved
Of Heaven, and blessed with sweet prosperity.
Look, eyes! rude hands have shorn our crested pride.
What see we now upon yon hill where late
Stood marble columns, atlasing a dome
Of porphyry? What see we in their stead?
Smoke-columns tremble in the wind, infirm.
The air is vacant of its loveliness.
O, last fair symbol of our early days,
Memorial of the simple saints of old,

Whose age men well call golden, for they lived
Amid the arcanal forest, in the ways
Of simple piety, and reaped the meed
Of piety, fair peace ; thou, on whose site
Stood that famed oracle of Aphrodite,
Wise as sublime Dodona, where the God
Speaks wisdom through his prophets.   Woe to them
That marred thee! woe to us, who, having left
The cloistered shades of the arcanal forest,
Rive and re-rivet to our needs the oak
That sheltered us, upbuilding haughty cities,
And, waxing strong, o'erween, nor bend our knees,
Nor beat our breasts in prayer, but lightly scoff
Such meek abasement!   Woe to us ! for God
Is mightier than the mightiest of men,
Mighty to bless his friends, mighty to lame
His enemies.   For midway in their course
Of pride, they stumble.   Death, remorse, defeat,
O'ertake them, or the rare eclipse is seen,
The visible frown of the invisible Lord.

I stand alone against a babbling host ;
But, being an ancient warrior of the Gods,

I fear them not. For God I stand. With God
They strive who strive with me. Most worthy judges,
The penalty of sacrilege is death.

  Lucius. Death? and for what, most reverend sire?
               Thyself
Must own I ever loved religion well,
That sweet religion which the Maker wrought
Into man's spirit, as the Arab girl
Weaves one rare golden thread amid the shawl
She weaveth of the smooth-shorn camel's hair.
All through the pattern rich it runs. Who plucks
That forth, unravels all. 'Tis true we burned
A sumptuous fane of frolic Aphrodite.
Home of carousals, consecrated plague,
What ceaseless sprinkling of prayer-perfumed waters
Could make thee pure? What incense hallow thee?
For this we merit honor, and not death.
Death? O most reverend sire and Senators,
Death for myself I fear not. I have faced
A thousand deaths, and count my life at nought
Against my country's peace. But here I stand
Pleading to-day, not for my life, but yours,
Lest in the spirit of party, and chagrin

For powers and honors by the Assembly's vote
Ta'en from you, — blind to the encircling perils,
Demosthenes without, famine within, — ye judge
To death the fifty captains, the sword-arm
Of Syracuse, now more than ever needful.
Look on the lots crisped careless in your hands.
What see ye there?   The lots?   No more?   Ye see
My living heart, but nought of that.   No more?
Ye see the lives of fifty noble youths,
Your own lives and your people's, and the life
Of Syracuse.   Go, cast them in the urn
That stands for Death.   Then bid the sentinels
Swing wide your gates asunder, that the foe
May march in o'er your bodies.   I am done.
   CHIEF SENATOR.   Is there no more to say?
                        May Justice light
Our minds, and guide us to the rightful path!
I weigh thy charge, Antenor, and thy words,
Young Lucius ; and my vote is cast for death.

*Uproar among the people and clash of arms.   Enter
Gylippus with a group of Spartans, and a Syracusan escort.*

GYLIPPUS.   Show me the generals.
GUARDSMAN.   Here.
GYLIPPUS.   It is a pretty pageantry ye hold.
Meanwhile a band of Spartan boys could scale
Your walls, and take your city.
CHIEF SENATOR.   Lord Gylippus!

The Senators rise.   The theatre becomes silent.

Welcome to Syracuse! our famed ally,
And kinsman by our Dorian ancestry.
Thou com'st upon us at an evil hour.
Well may the soldiers' discipline be lax
When they that govern them stand here accused
Of monstrous lawlessness.
GYLIPPUS.   At such an hour
I know but one crime, — treason.   It is met
With Death.
CHIEF SENATOR.   Mere treason injures only man.
Their deed, more black, offends the holy Gods.
Last night they burned a fane of Aphrodite,
And when we, with the noble priest, Antenor,
Sought to chastise them, turned their impious swords
On us, their elders.   But the miracle

Of Artemis cast terror on their hearts.
To-day thou seest them pleading for their lives,
Before the Senators of Syracuse,
Sole judges of the crime of sacrilege.

    LUCIUS.   Hear me, Lord!
We burned the fane. But know, the hand of hunger
Is at our throats, and, being the city's captains,
Commissioned by the Assembly with the powers
We held ere these proud Senators, now benched
In judgment over us, usurped them, — urged
By all the people, — we made bold to seize
The treasures of yon temple. This is the sum
Of our black conduct. We love Syracuse.
They love her Senate. Lord, thou art a soldier.
Then judge us as a soldier.

    GYLIPPUS.   I had done
The same, and smitten dead the meddling priest.
But smooth your own dispute, O Syracusans.
Demosthenes is at the gates. One breach
Of discord in your armor, and he enters.
I am a Spartan soldier, and can league
The strength of Sparta with no falling city.

    ANTENOR. Heed not the foreigner! The word of God

Is stronger on our side than Sparta's spears.
As ye have stood with me against the many
Before, stand with me now.   They must be ruled
Like children.

    CHIEF SENATOR.   Is there now no more to say?
Judges, ye hear accuser and accused,
And ye have heard Gylippus.   Rise in turn
And vote into the urns.   First, agèd Nestor.

    NESTOR.   None grieveth more than I to lose the fane,
For none but I remembers when 'twas built.
None honors thee, Antenor, more than I,
For zeal and holiness.   And yet, methinks,
Thou wast a hasty youth, and now, though white
With eld, thou still art hasty in thy zeal.
For, though thou lov'st thy temple, thou lov'st more
All Syracuse, and would'st not see that burned.
But if ye glare like enemies, and stand not
Like brothers, in a phalanx, how, alas!
How shall ye drive this mighty fleet away
That comes to seize our city?   So my vote
Is for forgiveness.   Else I know not how
The people can be calmed, and Lord Gylippus
Be won to lend us aid.

*He votes. A storm of approval among the people.
The rest follow Nestor, and vote, one by one, into
the urn of Pardon.*

CHIEF SENATOR. All see the judgment. Let the
  accused go free !
ANTENOR. Hold !
CHIEF SENATOR. What wouldst thou, Antenor ?
ANTENOR.   What would I ?
Shout ! Shout ! ye fools. I will not strive to out-
  roar ye.
What would I ? Perjured judges ! Heaven, restrain
Thy wrath, or visit it on wretched me !
For I am old, weak, useless to my people.
O let me wrap the cloak of solitude
About mine agèd head, and dwell apart.

The trial breaks up amid rejoicings of the people.

SCENE III.

At the gate of the Senate-House. The crowd has dispersed. Lucius and Gylippus, with guards, are leaving the theatre. Antenor follows them alone.

Enter, breathless, Adelia and Glauka.

ADELIA. Father!

ANTENOR. Adelia! My beloved child,
What brings thee here?

ADELIA. Barca — the drugs — last night,
Last night, — O, my bewildered brain!

GLAUKA. Last night
Our guest, Lord Barca, drugged her in the garden.

ANTENOR. Barca! ·

GYLIPPUS. What does the Punic general
In Syracuse?

GLAUKA. He left her on the beach,
Startled, I think, by sentinels. This morn
I found her there.

LUCIUS. Treachery! To the walls!
Three sentinels reported they pursued
Some foul deserter to the shore last night,
But lost him in the darkness.

Lucius approaches Adelia.

ANTENOR.   Go, rash youth!
Offend my sight no more; my daughter's sight
No more.
    LUCIUS.   O sire, hath ought escaped my lips,
Irreverent to thee?
    ANTENOR.   Away!
    LUCIUS.   O sire!
    ANTENOR. Away!
    ADELIA. What dost thou mean? Thou canst not
      mean
To sever me from Lucius?
    ANTENOR.   Stay the hand
Of doom I see in yonder heavens, uplift
O'er Syracuse. Then come and woo my daughter.

SCENE IV.

A month elapses. The Athenians are now in turn besieged in their camp at Plemmyrium by the Syracusans. The Athenian camp. A tent. Barca and Salander.

SALANDER.   Shake off this heavy spirit.
Thou art as variable, hast as many moods
As the chameleon colors.

BARCA.   I remember
Thou saidst I was inconstant. True! True! True!
My being had no centre till I knew
Adelia.

SALANDER.   If thou couldst forget the girl?

BARCA.   Forget her? Sooner shall Narcissus' flower
Erase the brand upon its cup than I
Her image on my heart.

SALANDER.   Thou art enchanted ;
But it was so with Hari ; 'twill be so
With her that ousts Adelia.

BARCA.   O Salander,
When I reflect upon the things I loved,
How like fair, brittle bubbles all appear,

Chased by a careless boy, caught, touched, and broken !
I loved our mighty city, when the throngs
Came forth, — each face a story to keen eyes, —
And darkened its white ways.   For I would dream
Some day they might be mine.
Were there a limner 'mid the fabled Gods
Not his aerial colors would suffice
To paint my vision's splendors.   But I wore
My giant will to nothing in the task,
And, baffled, fled to solitudes forlorn
And mountain steeps, whence man seems but a mote,
A speck upon the visible universe.
And yet sometimes the universe seems less
Than I, a speck, too, on the infinity
That I could cover were my spirit unsheathed,
And suffered to roam forth on wings of will.
I loved to dream upon a rolling meadow ;
I loved to wrap my spirit in the storm
And plunge through perils of the wind-swept sea.
Thus back and forth I went, as goes the bee, —
For we must go, — from flower to flower, from clime
To other clime.   I had a tryst in the vale,
A tryst in the highlands, and I kept them both

And made two maidens glad. I lived the warm,
Wild life ; yet oft I knelt before the shrines
In mystic meditation. Pleasure, love,
Song, war, ambition, Carthage, read the roll
Of my tributary joys, once fair and fragrant,
Now withered and flung off.
For midway in my course I met Adelia.
My being knew its centre ; as the leaves
Incline unto the light, I turned to her,
And now I see myself as to her eyes
I am, — endued with powers above all men,
Gigantic, yet unshapen, towering here
Above these Greeks, — a sculpture of the Nile
Beside a Phidian marble.

SALANDER.   Rouse thee! Yet
We may escape. Who knows?

BARCA.   Thrice we have failed,
Who never failed before. A strange despair
Deals icy stabs into my heart. Dost think
Men e'er have glimpses of their destiny?
We see the past, a memory-lighted wake,
Behind us ; are we then forever doomed
To break the foggy future as we go?

SALANDER.   There was an ancient soothsayer proph-
    esied
That I should die by steel.   But zounds!   I think
Death comes at random, and knows not himself
Or when or where.

BARCA.   Something here whispers to me
That I shall die in Syracuse.   Enough !
What tales are these dame Rumor sows in the air ?
Couriers fly back and forth ; the horses stamp ;
The soldiers whet their swords.

SALANDER.   Two captives, ta'en
This morn, guerillas from the inland countries,
Forewarn us of a general sea-assault
To-morrow.   O, for my old Numidian squadron !
These Greeks mistrust us, and I them.   Besides,
E'er since Gylippus came, the Syracusans
Are turned to Spartans.   They have trapped us here,
And swear we'll not escape them.   But what ho !
The bugle sounds a call ; from end to end
Of the long camp the answering trumpets ring.

            Bugle-calls.

BARCA.   To   arms, Salander !   Hear   the   mighty
    music.

This brooding is not life. I've seen a hound,
Tusked by the boar and bleeding, at my call
Leap back and charge one frantic onset more.
So let us charge against the throat of fate,
And hew a lane to liberty.

SALANDER.   Woe to the foe
That meets thee in this mood !

SCENE V.

The secluded garden. Glauka and Adelia.

Enter the High-Priest.

ANTENOR. Why, we neglect our garden. Weeds
    run wild
Among the flowers, and many stems are withered.
'Tis long since I have noticed them. Thou, Glauka,
Art paler than a maid of thy young years
Should ever be.

ADELIA.   I fear thou art not well
Thyself, dear father.

ANTENOR.   O, my sweet Adelia,
To gaze on thee, to sink this withered hand

Wrist-deep among thy golden curls, is cure
For my poor ailments.   Kiss me.   Thou art all
They leave me now, all that my people leave me.

ADELIA.   Nay, many messengers arrive each day
To ask for thee, and bring thee love and greeting.
One parted from us now, Lord Nestor's squire,
Who, as he bade good-speed, said "Bid thy sire
Rejoice ; the town is free."

ANTENOR.   The clouds of war
Are breaking round us.   Like two sister stars
That through a rifted storm shine forth in heaven
Shine ye serenely in your peaceful garden.

ADELIA.   And thou ?

ANTENOR.   I watch the morning grow to noon.
The noon to eve, and end my idle day
With sleep, more idle.

ADELIA.   Dost return so soon ?

ANTENOR.   Ay, to my chamber.   Fare you well
    awhile.

ADELIA AND GLAUKA.   Farewell !

ADELIA.   My father's hair is snowier.

GLAUKA.   Yes, lady, and his upright shoulders bend.

ADELIA. Why did he break with them? The people
    love him.
And he loves them, I know.

GLAUKA.   Two hearts may love
Whose faces are but as the faces of strangers.

ADELIA. What makes thee sad? I have not heard
    thee sing
This many a week.

GLAUKA.   In truth I am not happy.

ADELIA. If thou'st a sorrow, Glauka, pour it forth,
And we will cry together, solacing each
The other. For I, too, am melancholy;
But if I shut my grief within my heart,
'Twould eat a chasm there.

GLAUKA.   If I should tell,
Wouldst thou give promise never to reveal
My secret?

ADELIA.   If thou askest it, I will.
Now I remember Lucius often said,
"What shade is that, dwelling on Glauka's brow?"
And I could never tell.

GLAUKA.   Lucius?

ADELIA.   For when

Thou cam'st to me thou wast a stranger.   Since
Thou art become a friend.   But for the years
Before thou camest we are strangers still.
Sit by me on the bank, and let me be
Thy confidant.

GLAUKA.   It is an olden grief,
And the beginning of my tale is far,
Far back.   Then listen, lady.   Thou hast heard
Of Chios?

ADELIA.   Where Alcaeus flourished, one
Of those Ionian islands, that besprinkle,
Even like yon clouds, the Aegean isles of Heaven,
The ocean beyond Hellas toward the morn.

GLAUKA.   In Chios I was born.   There is my home.
Three sisters, fairer than myself, still watch
Our fireside embers there. -- Of all
The Chian youths, the fairest was my cousin,
Antinous, who dwelt beneath our roof.
Lithe was his frame, and smooth, and when he slept
His lips so rosy-ripe that mother Night
Would take them for a flower, and hang a drop
Of dew on them.   From early infancy
He played our island songs upon the lyre.

One day a wandering minstrel, hearing him,
Said to my sire, " Lord, thou art rich in lands,
But richer in this youth. Apollo's soul
Lives in him. At Olympia 'mid the best
Of Grecian minstrels I have seen a worse
Bear off the leafy prize." My sire resolved
To journey to the festival ; and we,
His daughters, went with fair Antinous,
Who played with me, and loved me, as a youth
Would love a maid ; and I loved him in turn,
But only as my playmate. When all Greece
Smiled on him from the tiers, he saw but me ;
For me he shook, with pleasure-lighted eyes,
The wreath he won. I looked beyond, and saw
Amon; the victors one who bore the wreath
For lyre and song, more noble than my cousin.
A flower in my bosom burst to bloom.
'Twas love.

   Soon, oh, too soon, the parting day
Arrived. My father said, " Home now to Chios ! "
I wept in secret, for I knew the youth
Dwelt far, — in Syracuse.

 ADELIA.   In Syracuse ?

GLAUKA.   And when he turned his forehead to the
    west,
How could I turn mine eastward, far from him
Forevermore?   I followed him by sea
To Syracuse.
    ADELIA.   Go on, my love,
    GLAUKA.   Alas!
He loved a lady there, fairer than I.
Whom when I saw, I marvelled not.   No goddess
Could rival her, not Aphrodite fair,
Nor Juno tall, nor Hebe with the cup
Of brimming youth, far sweeter than her wine.
I loved her, and she drew me to her side.
And round the pair, my lover and his love,
I hover, hiding in my bosom's deeps
My sorrow.   For my mien is never sad,
Though sometimes when I sing I give a voice
To secret, sad repinings.
    ADELIA.   His name? thy lover's name?
    GLAUKA.   Hast not divined it?
It is the name thy lip most loves to round.

Enter Lucius from behind the shrubbery.

Lucius. Adelia!

Glauka.　　　　　Oh! —

Adelia.　　　　Who calls me? Lucius? Heaven!

Lucius. Methought your very souls were in your
　　eyes,
Fair Glauka's raised to thine, thine drooping o'er them,
Like to the pale, calm blue of heaven bent o'er
The dark and troubled azure of the sea.
Thou hold'st thy matted hair to hide thy tears.
Glauka, what have I done?

Adelia.　　　　　Thou wast too sudden.
My sire forbade thee ever to see me more.

Lucius. Cruel Antenor! Plead with him, my love.
To-morrow's combat in the harbor marks
The doom of the Athenians. In their fleet
The traitorous Carthaginian, thrice foiled
Attempting to escape, fights like a God.
But I have sworn to have his life to-morrow,
And if the Gods are gracious, and we win,
Amid the general joy, — for still I think
No heart beats warmer for the city's weal
Than his, though now estranged, — might he not
　　then

Relent, Adelia ?   Speak !   I love thee more
A thousandfold than ever.

ADELIA.   Go, love, go.
I pray my father may not find thee here.

LUCIUS.   Brief are the stolen moments.   Speak one
  word
Of hope before I leave thee.

ADELIA.   Thou art rude.
Glauka, my loved companion, is not well.

LUCIUS.   Forgive me, I had eyes for nought but
  thee.

ADELIA.   Antenor must not see thee here.   The
  shock
Would shatter him.   Go, now, ere he returns.

LUCIUS.   Not yet, I cannot go.

ADELIA.   He comes, he comes.

LUCIUS.   To-morrow —

ADELIA.   Nay, I may not hear.

LUCIUS.   To-morrow, —
Tell him what I have told thee of to-morrow.

ADELIA.   Go, love.

Exit Lucius as Antenor re-enters.

ANTENOR.   My servant says the enemy strike
Their final blow for liberty to-morrow.
Defeated, they are lost.   Their hopes are dead,
And Syracuse is free.
     ADELIA.   God vouchsafe strength
To every soldier's arm !
     ANTENOR.   Amen !   Amen !
Be ready to go forth, and on the height
Above the harbor cheer the soldiers on,
And pray for Syracuse.
     ADELIA.   What !   I and Glauka ?
     ANTENOR.   We three.   Farewell.

Exit Antenor.

     ADELIA.   Glauka, art thou recovered ?
     GLAUKA.   Yes, lady, and I heard Antenor's words.
Sweet words !   But let me whisper something to thee.
Bend closer. — Wilt thou keep my secret ?
     ADELIA.   Yes.

Act Fifth.

Scene I.

Next morning. A height over the harbor. The fleet
anchored on the shore below. Enter the High-Priest,
with Glauka and Adelia.

ANTENOR.   Here let us stand,
And overlook the harbor.

GLAUKA.   O how fair!

ANTENOR.   It is a noble station whence to view
The island and the bay.   How smooth and calm
The water, as the sunshine trembles o'er it,
This lovely morn; more like some valley lake
That seems a patch of heaven's blue, fall'n on earth,
Than the wind-beaten ocean, fed with foam
Of submarine salt fountains.

ADELIA.   Such a day
Was never meant for war.   The gulls that here

Sport up and down the wind take not a thought
Of what is coming.   On their breasts they wear
No armor 'gainst their kind ; their talons clutch
No spears.   O God, to think that man to-day
Will stain the sea-green wave with scarlet blood
And heap it with corpses for the running tide
To cast upon the shore !

ANTENOR.   They come !   They come !

The army marches to the shore, below.

O hear the wild war-music.   By each band
The boyish minstrels march, and the feet of thousands
Beat to their martial measures.

ADELIA.   What a throng
Attends them to the shore !

ANTENOR.   Their brows are stern.
They all gaze out unto the foreign fleet
Across the harbor.   Many a soldier's eye
Is filled with tears.

GLAUKA.   And so are mine.

ANTENOR.   March on !
For he that overlives this victory

Shall wear a hero's crown, and he that falls
Shall have a grave within the memory
Of men, wet with the truest tears forever.

    ADELIA.   They grasp the ships and push them down
       the sands.
Some to the oars ; some poise their spears in air
Against an unseen foe.   Others draw bows,
Arrowless, but with sinewy, skilful arms.

    GLAUKA.   O, it is terrible ! I cannot think,
For all the tales of Asian amazons,
That women e'er were soldiers. It accords
With rough and cruel natures.

    ADELIA.   Nay, the sight
Arouses in my heart the wish that I
Could do a soldier's duty on the walls,
If Syracuse should call me.

    GLAUKA.   O, and sink
Thy hard spear in some foeman's tender breast,
And draw it out all red ?

    ANTENOR.   They are embarked,
And glide together from the crescent shore
With majesty.

ADELIA.   It is not like a battle ;
'Tis like a voyage of pleasure.
    ANTENOR.   Look afar !
The hostile fleet hath left its moorings.   See !
That long, dark line, midway across the harbor.
The wind is set against them.
    ADELIA.   Heaven be thanked !
    ANTENOR.   Now—now—they meet.   Hark ! Hark !
    ADELIA.   I hear a cheer
Borne o'er the water.
    ANTENOR.   'Twas the maiden shock.
Now they recoil.
    GLAUKA.   Can I not blind my eyes ?
My hands refuse to cover them.   Some charm
Rivets their gaze.
    ANTENOR.   The fleets break into clusters,
Some fly and some pursue.   The champion barks
Begin to single out each other.   Fierce
They battle round the centre of the fleet.
    GLAUKA.   I cannot tell the forms so far away.
Canst thou, Adelia ?
    ADELIA.   No, love.   But my eyes
Follow one ship.

GLAUKA.   Which one? Tell me a mark
That I may know it, and chain my glances to it
All through the day.
    ADELIA.   'Tis whiter than the rest,
It sails upon the left, as if it meant
To wheel around them.
    GLAUKA.   He is in it?
    ADELIA.   Yes.
My heart! That very trireme is attacked.
I thought I saw
A sailor aim a blow at one who stood
Before the rest. He missed. His shining blade
Is sheathèd in the sea.
    GLAUKA.   The other ships
Are come between them. I can see no more.
    ADELIA. Nor I.
    ANTENOR.   O gracious God of war,
Fight thou invisible with them, spread thy shield
Before them, lend them strength and surer aim.
Thou, God of Justice, bid the scales of Fate
Weigh true, against the foreign, false marauder,
Who crossed the sea, inveigled by sweet lure,
To snatch our city's plenty.

GLAUKA.   I must go.
I cannot bear to see the mangled ships,
And wrecks, and floating bodies.
        ANTENOR.   Nay, the fight
Is scarce begun as yet.   Our friends of Sparta,
Invincible on land, give way before
The Athenian's mariners.   Sit ye aside,
Turning your faces inland toward the hills,
And pray for Syracuse.   Here we remain
Until the day is over.

-------.

SCENE II.

Later.   Among the combatants.   Lucius' trireme.

LUCIUS.   O friendly mother night, make haste to fall
On this embattled ocean, far and wide
Bestrewn with desolation.   Spread thy veil
Of thickest gloom around us, that our fleet,
Now by the Athenian's desperate valor driven
So near the shore our dearest, watching there
Can spy our faces, yet may hold the foe
In strenuous combat till the early stars

Shall drive them, mangled, home, to rue the cost
Of this poor, barren victory.
  HELMSMAN.   Here comes
Barbaric Barca!   Ha! he swerves to strike
A galley from his path.   Look, how she sinks
Amid a bloody whirlpool.   Spears and shafts
Fly round his head, but like a tower he stands,
Unscathed, upon the prow.

  Barca comes in sight.   He is wounded in the breast.
     Salander dead at his feet.

  LUCIUS.   At last !   Die !   Die !
Infamous traitor !
  BARCA.   Whose bold challenge rings
Upon my shield ?
  LUCIUS.   O the tumultuous joy
To kill the evil snake that coiled his folds
About my sleeping darling !

    Sword-play.   Barca falls.

  LUCIUS.   So perish traitors !
  BARCA.   Was it thou, Adelia ?
I saw three forms erect upon yon heights,

With hands uplift in prayer, full darkly carved
Against the lighted sky.   Methought that thou
Wast one.   Thou first, Salander — Salander —
Adelia —

Dies.

HELMSMAN.   The African is dead.
LUCIUS.   And with her name on his unholy lips.
HELMSMAN.   I'd like to measure him from tip to tip,
As huntsmen measure some superb, large lion
After the chase is over.
LUCIUS.   Hark! the tide
Is changing while we linger.   Look! they fly!
They fly! To oars!

*A cheer from the Syracusan shore, answered by a dis-
tant wail from the Athenian onlookers across the
harbor.   The Athenians turn and fly.*

LUCIUS.   First board the Carthaginian,
Take off the crew and bind them!   Then row back
And charge full speed, and sink her in the sea.
Then —
HELMSMAN.   Master, art thou injured of a sudden?

LUCIUS. Some random arrow. Chance is the best
bowman.
The others could not hit me.
HELMSMAN. Pull it out.
Quick, men, and save Lord Lucius.
LUCIUS. Follow! Follow!
See the destroyers fleeing. Follow! Follow!
Like hounds behind the bounding stag, like Gods
Upon the heels of Titans. Follow! Follow!
HELMSMAN. Hush, master! for the wound is like a
fountain.
My tunic for a bandage.
LUCIUS. Do they fly?
The cheers are far ahead.
HELMSMAN. Yes, we are fallen
Behind the others.
LUCIUS. Cheer! my comrades, cheer!
This is the last of the Athenians,
And Syracuse is free.
HELMSMAN. Row for your lives.
A surgeon! O, a surgeon!

SCENE III.

*Evening.   Lucius dying on the shore.   The High-
Priest, Glauka, Adelia ; Soldiers and Sailors.*

ADELIA.   Hush! he is speaking.

LUCIUS.   Now the gorgeous light
Is sinking in the west.   For me not day,
But time, is setting, and eternity,
The starless night, ariseth.

ADELIA.   Lucius, say
Thou knowest me.

LUCIUS.   The twilight of a forest,
How vast and calm!   Men pass.   Their forms grow
          vague,
Dissolve, and leave no outline to the eye.
Is this a land 'twixt life and death, through which
I journey to my goal?   But lo! a shape
Of glory waits me, radiant as the sun,
When Vesper at Heaven's gate points east and west
Her clarion, and convenes the roaming Gods
To hoar Olympus to the mighty feast,
And Phoebus sinks in splendor.   It draws near.

Come, let me grasp thee, bathe my soul in thee.
Ha, was it thou, Adelia?

O my love,
How rich with life, like a full fruit, art thou!
Thy dewy eyes, thy sweetly grieving lips,
Thy poise erect and womanly, thy frame
Made for caresses.   Darling, wilt thou do
My dying wish?

ADELIA.   Were it to do the deeds
Of Hercules, or shake the world.

LUCIUS.   Be happy!

ADELIA.   O love, thou askest what I cannot do.
My heart, the fountain-spring from which joy bubbles,
Is frozen to a stone.   My lips are marble.
How shall I ever smile again?

LUCIUS.   Be happy.
And in the years to come, when soothing Time
Hath healed thy heart, when, standing in the stream
Of joy, up to thy lips, — the golden stream
That flows through mortal life eternally, —
Thou canst but drink again and smile, — 'twill be
A happy sorrow to remember me.
Remember me when autumn seres the fields,

And pity for the yellowing leaves of summer
Comes o'er thee with the season : when the dusk
Drives daylight from the garden, and night winds
'Gin mourn, remember me ! remember me
When far-away, soft music fills the air
And floods thy spirit with a mingled draught
Of rapturous aches and pleasures.   Then, Adelia,
Remember Lucius.

ADELIA.   O, my heart is breaking.
The happy by-gones — are they dead forever?

ANTENOR.   I was too stern ; forgive me.

LUCIUS.   Is it thou,
Antenor?   Come more near, and take my hand.
Do not accuse thyself.

ANTENOR.   Thou goest to meet
The bridegroom, Death, to whom thou wast betrothed
The day that thou wast born.   Dark powers place
Our infant hands in his, and while men say
"Another life " they say "Another death."
But blest are they, the fearless and the good,
To whom Death comes in raiment of the dawn,
With gentle visage, Love upon his right,
And glory on his left.   Whose last looks see

The loving faces round them ; whose last sounds
Are words of whispered comfort. In thine ears
A paean is resounding, sung afar
By thy victorious comrades, disembarking.
Hark to the shouts, the clash of arms, the cries
Of welcome, and the laughter, and the songs,
And shriller accents when sweet children blend
Their joyous jargon. 'Tis the mingled hymn
Of our thanksgiving. Let these things assuage
Thy pain. Thy rescued country honors thee.

Triumphal music.

Lucius (*rousing*). Rejoice, O Syracuse, at this
    grand hour
Triumphal, in thy valor and thy strength !
In thy war-weary legions that return   .
Within thy peaceful bosom ! O rejoice
In thy sea-girdled beauty, now set free
From marring foes ! Rejoice in thy blue sky !
Thy forts and armories, thy marts and shrines,
Thy cots and bowers and citadels ! Rejoice
In thy fair history, writ not on rolls

Of parchment, but on more unfading leaves,
Thy sons' brave eyes, the pure cheeks of thy daughters.
Thine elders' reverend miens!

My Syracuse!

Dies.

www.ingramcontent.com/pod-product-compliance
Lightning Source LLC
Chambersburg PA
CBHW032147010726
47493CB00008BA/2623